Pick,
Peck
through the top.
Push,
poke,
out I

POP!

Pauline Poulet

Growing, growing,
chick to hen.
I cluck triumphant,
CLUCK AGAIN!

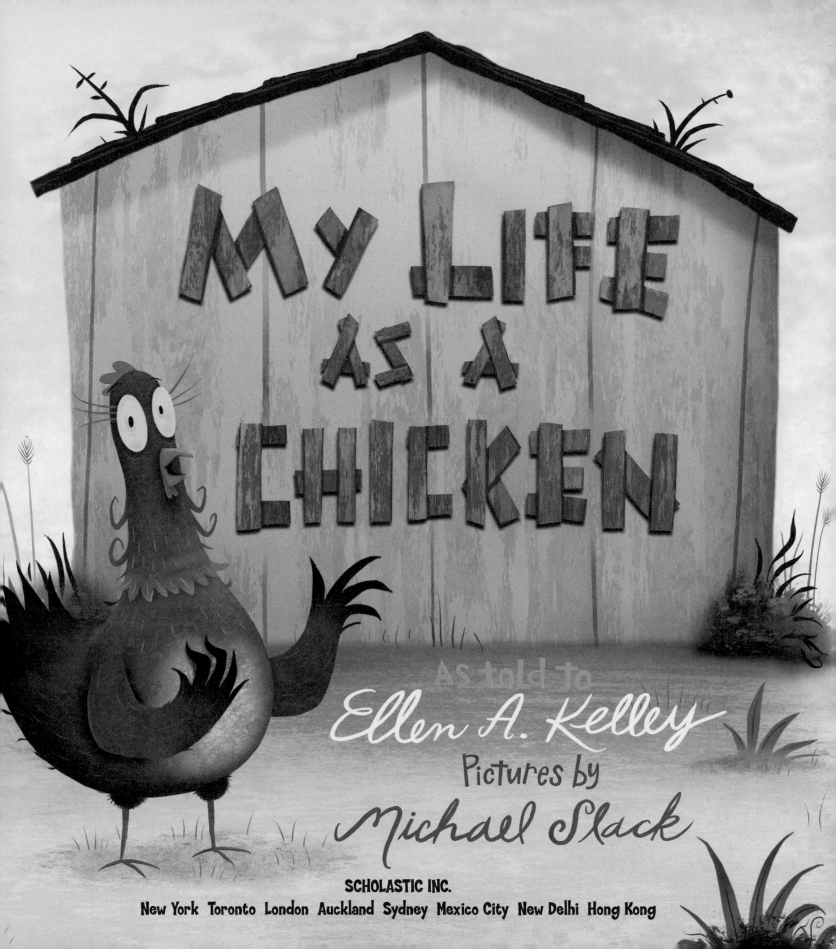

My Life as a Chicken

As told to
Ellen A. Kelley

Pictures by
Michael Slack

SCHOLASTIC INC.
New York Toronto London Auckland Sydney Mexico City New Delhi Hong Kong

ISBN 978-0-545-24224-0

Text copyright © 2007 by Ellen A. Kelley.
Illustrations copyright © 2007 by Michael Slack.
All rights reserved. Published by Scholastic Inc.,
557 Broadway, New York, NY 10012, by arrangement with Houghton Mifflin Harcourt
Publishing Company. SCHOLASTIC and associated logos are trademarks and/or
registered trademarks of Scholastic Inc.

12 11 10 9 8 7 6 5 4 3 2 1   10 11 12 13 14 15/0

Printed in the U.S.A.   08

First Scholastic printing, February 2010

The illustrations in this book were done digitally using mixed media.
The display lettering was created by Michael Slack.
The text type was set in Coop and Potato Cut.
Designed by Lauren Rille

For John and our family
For Julia, in keeping my promise
For Jean and all those who helped me prevail—E. K.

To Phyllis L. Michaels (the best grandma ever),
with thanks for teaching me so many things and encouraging
all of my oddball childhood creative endeavors—M. S.

On my nest I sit, spellbound.
Underneath me I have found,
perfect, smooth, and almost round,
my first,

my lovely

EGG.

Hard at work I cluck 'n' lay
night and day—no time to play.
Laying dozens is my fate,
eggs in cartons, eggs in crates.

I'll be his special of the day
at Cock-a-Doodle-Doo Café!

HENS, AWAY!

Out the gate,
I must escape
the dinner plate!

To the brooding woods I scramble,
prickly briar'd, bristly brambled.
I am chased by hungry brutes.
I am spooked by swoopy hoots.

I squeeze inside a log to hide.
Fox is mad. He's stuck outside.
He snarls and snaps.
I flinch and flail,
then raise my cry,

"Pauline,
Prevail!"

Now a windy whip-and-twirl
sucks us up inside its swirl,
then spits us out:
Fox, log, and me.
I tumble to
CATASTROPHE.

...to the sea, dunked and washed,
almost drowned, soppy-sloshed.

Then pirates pull me
from the foam.

Why, oh why,
did I leave home?

I polish brass and sweep the scupper,
but Captain wants me for his supper.
The ship's cook reaches for my neck!
I flap fast past the quarterdeck.

By sneaking off this shifty ship,
I'll give these scalawags the slip.
Hours pass atop the mast.
I wait.
The sea cats snooze at last!

Yawn

I tiptoe aft, steal a raft,
brave the waves,
and sail my craft.

I face the fearsome typhoon's wail, clucking loud,

"Pauline, Prevail!"

I am tossed, tail over beak,
landing hard, a wet-hen heap,
in something bobbing on the tide:
a basket—dry, unoccupied.

WHAT NOW?

A pull, a lift, surprising!
From the water I am rising,
crossing sea, skimming moon,
carried by a big balloon.

I navigate high altitudes,
an aeronaut with fortitude.
Above me burns a blaze of stars,
below the view blurs fast and far.
One hen aloft, so all alone—

WiLL I eveR
find A home?

From the corner of my eye,
I spy a speck high in the sky.
It circles closer, then arrives—

A
HAWK!

I duck.

Claws out, it dives.

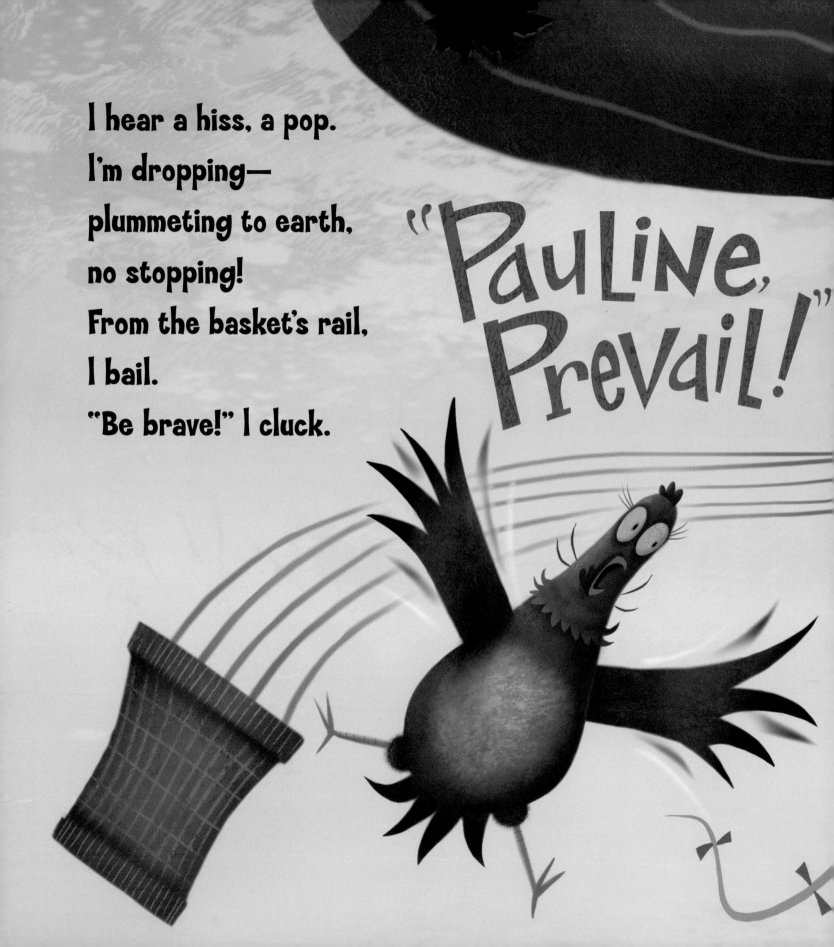

I hear a hiss, a pop.
I'm dropping—
plummeting to earth,
no stopping!
From the basket's rail,
I bail.

"Be brave!" I cluck.

"Pauline,
Prevail!"

Then coming fast,
hard on the right,
I see a paper bird.
A kite!
We meet.
I leap and latch on tight.

I ride the kite,

cling and swing,

wilted, wounded,
weak of wing,

then fall, crashing hard and steep,
deep into chicken sleep.

Whispers wake me, gentle, shy.
Cradled, smoothed, and soothed am I,
carried somewhere safe and warm:
a soft straw bed near coops of corn.

I've found a paradise for me:
new friends, new nest, new family.
My new home is this petting zoo.

Now, wouldn't you?